Lions

The Mill Pond Ghost
and other stories

Pamela Oldfield

The
Mill Pond Ghost
and other stories

Illustrated by
David Senior

Lions
An Imprint of HarperCollinsPublishers

The Mill Pond Ghost and other stories
was first published in 1991 in Lions
Second impression June 1992

Lions is an imprint of
HarperCollins Children's Books,
part of HarperCollins Publishers Ltd,
77–85 Fulham Palace Road, Hammersmith,
London W6 8JB

ISBN 0 00 694090-0

Printed and bound in Great Britain by
HarperCollins Manufacturing, Glasgow

Contents

THE
MILL POND
GHOST

The Mill Pond Ghost

The new camera was exactly what Steven had always wanted – an instamatic with built in flash for dark days or interiors. With the camera there were two free films, one black and white, the other colour. The camera was second prize in a raffle and Steven was glad he had not won first prize because that was a fishing rod and he was not the least bit interested in fishing. He had never won a raffle before and probably never would again but he had the camera and that was all that mattered. Now he could join the school camera club. Andrew and Bob, his two friends, had been members for ages and they seemed to enjoy it.

His sister Sandra said, "You can take a photo of me if you like," but Steven shook his head.

"I'll go for a walk," he said, "and look for some landscapes."

Sandra looked puzzled so he explained. "A landscape is a view," he said. "The camera club runs competitions. Last month it was about animals but this month it's landscapes."

Saturday morning found Steven ready and waiting to go at five past eight. His mother had made him some sandwiches and she put them into his haversack with a bottle of milk and a couple of apples.

"And stay away from the mill pond," she reminded him. "You know what they say about it. You know about Alice Browning."

"Oh Mum!" he groaned. "That's just a story. Nobody really believes in ghosts. I certainly don't."

"Well, stay away anyway," she insisted. "Just to please me."

He promised reluctantly and wished his mother had not mentioned it because he had planned to take a photograph of the pond.

He set off at last and began to enjoy himself. He had put a black and white film in the camera and soon found his first subject – a view across the fields to an old church. Next he photographed a tumbledown barn framed between two oak trees and then a herd of cows grazing in a field of tall grass.

By this time he was feeling hungry so he sat down on a stile between two fields and started to eat his sandwiches. Lettuce and tomatoes – his favourites!

"Good old Mum!" he murmured.

It was a pity about the mill pond, he reflected. It was less than a quarter of a mile away and would have made a marvellous picture with the trees reflected in the water. But if he did take one his mother would see the photograph and then she would make a fuss.

"It's not worth it!" he told himself with a shrug. Then he shivered and began to wish he had brought an anorak. He would have to get properly organized next time.

Plenty of people had claimed to see the mill pond ghost but Steven put it down to imagination and could not take it seriously. The postman claimed to have seen it three times in all. He described it as a woman in a long dress with a shawl over her head. According to him it was definitely Alice Browning, the young servant from the manor house who had drowned in the pond seventy years ago.

The story was that she had been jilted by her sweetheart, Albert – the miller's older son. Crazy with grief the unfortunate girl had thrown herself into the rushing water. At that time, of course, the mill had been working and the great wheel had churned through the water to turn the machinery which ground the corn. Her body had been found by the miller the next morning. Steven had seen her grave in the churchyard.

Now the deserted mill was derelict, a gloomy, brooding place and most people were quite happy to stay away from it. It would make such a super photograph, thought Steven and suddenly he decided that, in spite of his mother's warning, he would take a photograph of the mill.

Impulsively he jumped to his feet and set off along the overgrown path that led to the mill. He shivered again and glanced up at the sky, thinking it must have clouded over. But no. The sun still shone and yet with every step he took he felt colder and colder.

Steven hesitated. Around his feet last year's dead leaves were lifted into the air by a chill wind.

"It's nothing," he told himself. "I'm imagining things."

He went on but now he noticed that the birds had stopped singing. In their place he heard a noise like rushing water.

"It can't be," he insisted and after a moment's hesitation he pressed on.

The air grew colder still as the noise of rushing water grew closer and then something happened which made his hair stand on end. He heard the sound of someone sobbing! A wild, abandoned sobbing, full of anguish and despair.

Even then Steven refused to believe that he was in the presence of the supernatural.

"Who's there?" he called out and his voice quavered a little. "What's the matter?"

There was no answer to his questions and with a beating heart he forced himself to walk on until he rounded the corner. Now the mill itself appeared before him, dark and forbidding, its windows open to the elements, its brickwork crumbling. Beside it the mill pond was stagnant and full of weeds but still the sound of rushing water filled the air, louder than ever and above that the pitiful sobbing continued.

He called again. "Where are you?"

Suddenly a woman's voice cried out. "Oh Albert! Albert! How could you forsake me?"

The sound came from somewhere near the water but there was no one to be seen.

Thoroughly frightened, Steven adjusted his camera and took a quick shot of the mill beyond the water. His teeth were chattering with a mixture of cold and fear and his hands trembled as he pressed the button.

Then he turned and ran.

By the time he got home three hours later Steven had recovered from his fright and decided to say nothing about his adventure. When he took the film into the chemist to be processed he had forgotten all about it.

He collected the photographs on the following Wednesday and opened the packet with a thrill of pleasure. Would one of them be good enough to enter in the competition?

He flicked through them until he came to the one taken by the old mill.

As he looked at it a shudder of disbelief ran through him. By some miracle the film had not blurred. The mill stood out dark and sombre above the smooth water but beside the water there was a shadowy figure.

"It can't be!" whispered Steven. "There was no one else there! I was on my own!"

But was he? There in the photograph was the figure of a young woman. She was wearing a long dress – and her head was covered by a shawl.

Steven had photographed the mill pond ghost!

THE BOY
IN THE WOOD

The Boy in the Wood

John, Peter and Ian were picnicking in the little wood between the two farms. They had eaten all the food and Peter was finishing off the last mouthful of orange squash.

John looked at his watch. "Five past seven," he told them.

"Who cares?" replied Ian. "We're not going anywhere, are we?"

Ian was eleven, rather tubby with ginger hair. John, his cousin, was twelve, taller and thinner. Peter was eleven years old exactly. It was his birthday and the picnic had been his choice of a celebration. He was fair with freckles.

"I'm FTB," he announced.

The other two stared at him.

"FTB?" echoed John. "What's FTB?"

"Full to Bursting," Peter told him. "My uncle says it every year after Christmas dinner."

"Your uncle sounds a bit daft to me," said Ian but he did not mean it unkindly. Ian thought all grown-ups were "a bit daft".

17

Peter smiled. "And my aunt says 'God bless my stomach!'"

Ian groaned. "What a hilarious family. You have my sympathy."

John sat up a little straighter and wiped crumbs from his mouth with the back of his hand.

"Ten past seven," he told them.

Ian and Peter grinned. John had had the watch for his birthday a few weeks earlier and the novelty had not yet worn off. He insisted on telling them the time every few minutes in spite of their teasing.

They screwed up the wrapping papers and stuffed everything back into the haversack.

"Your turn to carry it," John told Ian.

"I know. You don't have to tell me."

They sat in lazy silence for a few more minutes and then Ian stretched his arms and stood up.

"We've got time for one more game," he said. "I vote one of us hides and the others hunt him down."

John said, "Hide and seek? But that's kids' stuff."

"Not hide and seek," Ian explained. "One of us is the terrorist who has just blown up a bridge or something and the other two are the security forces." Put that way it sounded a bit more exciting.

18

"I don't think I've got the energy," said Peter. But his friends insisted that it was too early to go home.

"And we can't just sit here like lemons," said John.

"It will soon be dusk," Ian added, "and the wood's quite creepy in the dark. Anything could happen."

It was agreed. Peter volunteered to be the terrorist and the others decided to give him three minutes in which to find a hiding place.

"Twenty-five past seven," said John. "We'll be coming at seven twenty-eight precisely! Synchronize your watches everyone."

Peter grinned, then ran off through the trees, zigzagging as he went to throw his companions off his trail.

He made his way to a hollow tree which was one of his favourite places. The top half of the tree had fallen years ago when it was struck by lightning and it had rotted over the years. Brambles grew around it but Peter knew that there was a gap in the middle that was not visible from the outside.

He was pushing his way through the brambles when he stopped in surprise.

A boy was sitting in his special place, leaning back against the tree.

"Oh – sorry!" said Peter, surprised.

19

"It's OK," said the boy.

He looked vaguely familiar but Peter was sure he did not live in their village.

The boy moved over. "There's room for two," he said with a smile.

Peter hesitated. "I'm with some mates," he said. "They'll be looking for me in a minute."

"I know."

The boy was fair haired with grey eyes and looked about the same age as Peter. Peter sat down facing him and said "My name's – " Before he could finish the boy said "Peter."

"How do you know that?" Peter asked curiously. There was something strange about the boy – something he could not place.

"I just do."

"What's yours then?"

"Robert."

"I suppose they call you Bob."

The boy looked away suddenly. "No," he said quietly. "They don't call me anything."

For a moment neither of them spoke.

Peter said, "At any moment John and Ian will come crashing through the wood, looking for me. I'm supposed to be a terrorist and they're the security forces. It's just a silly game really."

Robert looked at him blankly but made no comment. Suddenly he said "Oh, I nearly forgot. Happy birthday, Peter."

Peter tried to hide his confusion. "How did you know? I mean we don't know each other. I don't know your birthday."

The boy sighed deeply and Peter thought he looked sad. But he did not answer the question. Instead he said, "It's nice here. I often come to this little hollow. I wait for you."

"You wait for me?" Peter stared at him. "But I never see you. And why me?" He drew a deep breath. "Look, what are you on about?" he said crossly. "You're not making any sense. I've never seen you before and yet you –"

"It doesn't matter," said the boy quickly and now his lips trembled as though he was going to cry. "I shouldn't have come. It's my fault. Don't be angry, Peter." He stood up and Peter at once regretted his irritation. He, too, jumped to his feet and opened his mouth to apologise but the boy was shaking his head.

"Don't say any more," he said. "I know how you feel but I had to come. I had to talk to you – just once. We won't meet again but remember – I often come to this little hollow. I'm often here, waiting for you but you won't see me again."

Then, to Peter's astonishment, he stepped forward, threw his arms around Peter's neck and hugged him fiercely. Suddenly, without knowing why, Peter found himself returning

21

the hug. He felt too choked to speak and there were tears in his eyes.

When at last they drew apart the boy said, "Goodbye, Peter."

Peter found his voice and said, "Don't go! Please don't go. Not yet!"

But Robert shook his head. "I have to go," he said sadly. He turned and began to stumble away through the trees. Peter called after him. "I won't forget you, Robert!" But by that time the boy had disappeared among the trees.

As soon as Peter went into the kitchen Mum knew that there was something wrong.

"Peter!" she cried. "You look as white as a sheet! Whatever is the matter?"

Peter shook his head and sank down on to a chair. His father came in from the garden and he, too, stared at his son's white face.

"What's up, son?" he asked.

Mum said, "He's like a ghost. I'm just trying to find out what's happened."

Slowly, Peter began to tell his strange story. When he reached the part where the boy told him his name his mother gave a strangled cry.

"Robert? Oh no, it can't be!" she whispered and now she was pale and trembling. His father, too, looked shaken by the story. "Go on, son" he said quietly.

Wonderingly Peter finished the account but by this time his mother was crying. Peter looked from one to the other. "What does it mean, Dad?" he asked.

His father put an arm round his wife. "It means you met your twin brother," he said. "Don't ask me how because I don't know the answer. But that's who it was, Peter. Your twin brother, Robert."

Peter's eyes widened with shock.

"But I haven't got a twin brother!" he protested. "I'm an only child. You know I am!"

His father shook his head. "When you were born you were a twin," he said softly, "but your brother died an hour after he was born. It was terrible. We were so unhappy that we just could not speak of it. We didn't like to remember that we should have had two sons." He sighed deeply and Peter's mother took up the tale. "By the time you were old enough to understand there didn't seem any point in telling you and upsetting ourselves all over again. Perhaps it was a mistake but it seemed best at the time."

Peter stared at them for a moment then stammered, "You mean I saw my twin brother's ghost!"

"Yes," said Dad. "It must have been Robert. That's how he knew your birthday. It would have been his birthday too."

Mum had stopped crying. Now she said, "No wonder you thought you recognized him! He must have looked just like you! You were so alike – like two peas in a pod, as they say."

Peter frowned. "Of course! He did look like me but I didn't realize."

While Dad made a pot of coffee Mum made him tell the story again and asked him dozens of questions. Then they all walked round to the churchyard and Peter saw his brother's grave for the first time. There were fresh flowers on it but it was so small. A baby's grave.

"Poor Robert," said Peter sadly.

"And poor you," said Dad. "You would have had a lot of fun with a brother. Still, you've got plenty of friends. Poor Robert has no one."

"He felt so real," said Peter. "When he hugged me, I mean. It's almost worse now that I've met him because now I know what we've lost."

Mum nodded. "Still," she said, "you know he is often at the hollow. He told you that. When you go there you can imagine he's there even if you can't actually see him."

They walked home in a thoughtful silence.

Peter went regularly to the hollow after that and he, too, put flowers on Robert's grave. He might never see his twin brother again – that much he knew. But he would never give up hoping.

SIMON ATTLEY'S
DESK

Simon Attley's Desk

Simon sat on his desk in the back row of the classroom. On it.

He sat cross-legged and watched the door as the first of the children wandered in. The first lesson was maths. Simon said, "One seventeen is seventeen, two seventeens are thirty-four, three seventeens are fifty-one, four seventeens are sixty-eight . . ."

John came in first followed by Steve and Charlie and then Sue came in, arm in arm with Wendy, her "soul mate". More children crowded into the room and the class teacher followed them in. His name was Mr Burkey but for obvious reasons the children had nick-named him Turkey. He carried a pile of exercise books and began to give them out, tossing them on to the desks with practised ease. At the same time he said, "Steve, clean the board please."

Steve went up to the blackboard and began to rub off some history notes about King Alfred.

Simon sighed. Turkey never asked him to clean the board. Not any more.

Dan Hatter sat down in the desk next to Simon but they did not speak to each other. Dan was "a bit of a twit" in Simon's opinion and they didn't like each other. Never had.

Soon all the desks were occupied and the teacher called the register and for once no one was absent. He began to write long division sums on the blackboard and Simon watched him silently. Turkey was OK, he thought. A bit boring but OK. Better than some of the staff. Better than Mr Harper the headmaster.

He glanced down at the desk lid on which he sat and saw his initials carved in one corner. SA for Simon Attley. Simon smiled. He was feeling happier already.

The lesson began and soon all the children were hard at work, their heads bent over their books, scribbling industriously. Simon liked maths. He was good at it. He could do the work quicker than any of the others. He was already on the fourth sum. He did it in his head. Two thousand five hundred and forty four divided by twelve was two hundred and twelve. Simple.

Turkey walked up the aisle between the desks, looking at each child's work and pointing out where they were going wrong.

To Wendy the teacher said, "You've got the right answer but the working out's wrong. Do it again and think!" Behind his back Wendy put out her tongue.

Dan Hatter leaned forward and stuck the point of his biro into the neck of the boy in front. Andy squealed loudly and his hand shot up into the air. "Sir! Sir! Dan Hatter stabbed my neck!"

Dan stared up at the teacher with a look of great innocence. "Me sir? I didn't, sir! Honest I didn't!"

Simon sighed. It was the stupid sort of thing Dan would do. He gave him a scornful look but Dan ignored him.

Turkey said, "Get on with your work, Andy, and stop fussing."

At that moment the classroom door opened and the headmaster came in with a girl they had not seen before.

She had fair hair which she wore in a single plait and she carried a school bag under her arm. She looked very nervous and Simon's good mood faded. There was nowhere for the girl to sit. Mr Harper looked round the class and all the children were silent.

"This is Louise Carter," he announced. "She has just moved to this area from Chester. I hope you will all do your best to make her feel at home." He gave her a brief smile, nodded to Turkey and left the room.

At once Steve put up his hand. "Sir, where's she going to sit? There's no spare desk."

Simon nodded his agreement but the girl

registered surprise at this remark and Turkey looked a bit upset. Simon watched them angrily. Not again, he thought. Didn't teachers ever learn?

"Nonsense," said Turkey. "She can sit there at the back."

The classroom was utterly silent, shocked. Then the children began to whisper among themselves.

Andy said, "But sir! Couldn't we bring in another desk? There are a few spare ones in the library."

Turkey looked positively flustered now. "We don't need another desk. There's one already empty."

In a scared voice Wendy said, "But sir, that's – that's Simon's desk. Simon Attley."

Turkey gave Wendy a warning look and pointed to Simon's desk. "You can sit there," he told the new girl with a tight smile.

Obediently she walked along the aisle as Simon slid from the desk and stood beside it. All eyes were on the girl as she sat down.

Dan said, "But sir, she'll – that is - Oh sir, remember what happened to Adrian!"

All the children began to talk at once. They all remembered only too well.

Quickly Turkey said, "That's quite enough talking. All get on with your work or you'll stay in at dinnertime." He gave the new girl a book and told her to make a start on the sums that he had written on the blackboard.

Simon watched her, his face furious. Within minutes she began to shiver.

"Please Mr Burkey," she asked, "May I fetch my anorak. I'm so terribly cold."

Turkey's face was very white. He hesitated then asked, "Cold? In the middle of August?"

"But I am, sir!" she insisted.

Simon smiled but all eyes were on the new girl.

"Is anyone else cold?" asked Turkey.

"No sir!" they chorussed.

When he spoke his voice was almost a whisper. "No one else is cold."

She said, "I'm sorry Mr Burkey, but I'm freezing!" Her teeth were chattering.

Turkey gave in. "Fetch it if you must," he told her and she left the room.

Simon stared round him at all the frightened faces. What a lot of softies they were, he thought dispassionately. He waited for the girl to come back. She was wearing a new regulation blue anorak with the school badge on the top pocket. Without an "Excuse me" she pushed past Simon and sat down again. For a moment she stared at the initials he had carved and then she ran her fingers very slowly over the letters. First the "S", then the "A".

Simon's eyes narrowed. He snatched her maths book from the desk and threw it across the room. It hit the door and dropped to the floor. There was a terrified gasp from the class and someone started to cry. Even Turkey looked frightened. The new girl gave a scream of fear, leaped from the desk and ran to the front of the class.

After a long silence Wendy said, "It was Simon, sir!" Her voice trembled.

All eyes were turned to the back of the room where Simon was standing with his arms folded.

The girl said, "Who's Simon?" but nobody answered her question.

Several of the other children were beginning to shiver now and a strong cold draught swept the room and rattled the window panes. A few loose papers flew into the air and Wendy covered her eyes with her hands. Sue began to whimper and Dan closed his eyes and began to gabble The Lord's Prayer.

Steve said urgently, "Sir! Couldn't we please fetch her another desk? You know what happened to Adrian Mitcham!"

The new girl looked at the teacher and then turned to a boy sitting in the front row. "What did happen to him?"

The boy whispered, "He nearly went mad. The doctor said – "

Turkey snapped, "Stop that whispering." To

the boy he said, "You will stay in at dinner-time."

"But sir! I've got football practice!"

"That's not my problem," said Turkey. He was beginning to recover, thought Simon.

The new girl said fearfully, "Please, Mr Burkey, could I sit somewhere else?"

He hesitated. "There is nowhere else," he told her. He swallowed hard and added, "And there is nothing wrong with that desk at the back. I refuse to believe– "

But all around him the children joined in a noisy chorus of disbelief.

"Please, Mr Burkey, don't make her sit there!"

"Sir, that's Simon Attley's desk!"

"Sir, Adrian Mitcham was – "

"Sir, you know what will happen!"

"Oh sir, please – "

Simon remained unmoved by the hubbub. He stood beside his desk working out the last sum on the blackboard. "Seven thousand seven hundred and twenty eight divided by twenty four equals . . . " He closed his eyes. He always concentrated better with his eyes closed. "Three hundred and twenty two!"

He had a fantastic brain where figures were concerned. The school had called him a mathematical genius. They had told his parents that there was a spectacular career ahead of him, maybe in electronics. Maybe in the world of banking. Or in the government as an adviser. But first he must pass his exams. The noise in the classroom was suddenly interrupted by a loud bell.

The children, relieved, jumped to their feet, but Simon scowled. The new girl had wasted most of the maths lesson and now it was art. He had never been good at art.

Without a word he stood at the back of the room and watched the rest of the class file out into the corridor.

No one spoke to him but he did not care. He was used to it.

He saw Turkey speaking to the new girl and finally saw the teacher nod his head.

So, thought Simon. They would be getting her another desk after all. A good thing too. He hated sharing.

Outside in the corridor Wendy and Sue had "adopted" the new girl. Together the three of them walked along the corridor towards the art room.

"You'll like the art teacher," said Wendy with studied cheerfulness. "Her name's Miss Griffiths. She's fun."

The new girl was not listening. "What did happen to Adrian Mitcham?" she asked.

Wendy lowered her voice. "He had a terrible time. Turkey sat him in Simon Attley's desk and awful things kept happening to him. He was terrified. He was always terribly cold, like you. One day last term he simply refused to come to school. He began to have nightmares and was afraid to go to sleep at night. It made him ill – in his mind. In the end his parents took him away and sent him to another school."

"But who is this Simon Attley?"

Sue said, "He's a boy. He used to be in our class."

Wendy said, "He still *is* in our class!"

Sue frowned at her friend. "Well, I suppose he is in a way. At least his ghost is. Poor Simon. He wasn't a very easy boy to get to know but he was absolutely brilliant at maths."

Wendy nodded. "We were all out tobogganing one day last winter and suddenly he collapsed and died. From the cold, they said."

Sue said, "One minute he was laughing and the next minute – " She left the sentence unfinished.

"Now his ghost haunts the school," said Wendy. "At least he haunts our classroom. We all know he's there but the staff won't admit it. Not that anybody's actually seen him but we know he's here by what he does. You saw that book today." The new girl nodded, and Wendy went on, "We're not supposed to talk about it in case it gives the school a bad name."

After a moment the new girl said, "Mr Burkey

says I can have one of the spare desks from the library."

"Good," said Wendy. "You'll be OK. Just try and forget what happened this morning. Simon's OK as long as nobody tries to take his desk."

They reached the art room and the new girl hung back.

"Will he be in here?" she asked nervously.

"Oh no," they told her. "He doesn't like art."

When the classroom had emptied, Simon climbed back on to the desk.

His desk.

The one with his initials carved on the lid. Seeing those initials made him feel good. SA for Simon Attley. No one who saw them could ever say that Simon Attley did not exist. He sat cross-legged and prepared to wait for the next maths lesson. Tomorrow at ten thirty. He was looking forward to that.

THE
WHITE KILLER

The White Killer

The snow came suddenly, just after seven a.m. I did not expect it. It came down in large flakes which fell thickly and began to settle. It snowed all day.

By eleven that night a breeze had sprung up and that made it worse because it caused the snow to form drifts – deep drifts into which a person could stumble unawares.

Then it stopped snowing and the clouds rolled away and the full moon lit up the smooth, white landscape.

By this time I was numb with cold and hardly able to drag myself along. My feet were frozen and my hair was spiked with snow. I had eaten nothing since the morning when a kindly farmer's wife had thrown me a crust from her kitchen window.

Suddenly I saw a light through the trees to my left and with a last effort stumbled towards it. A light meant people and people meant help, however limited.

I struggled to the door and reached for the

knocker. A new brass knocker in the shape of a lion's head.

Rat-a-tat-tat!

For a long time nothing happened but I knew the house was occupied by the lighted windows.

I tried again.

Rat-tat!

Finally the door opened and a girl stood in the doorway, a cautious look on her face. I took her to be about eleven. Behind her I saw two younger children.

"What do you want?" she asked.

"Shelter," I began. "Warmth. A little food –" I swayed and almost fell and she put out a hand to steady me.

"Who is it?" asked one of the other children.

The girl said, "It's a girl. She wants to come in."

A boy appeared beside her. "Mum said we were not to let anyone in," he said.

"Please!" I begged. "Let me speak with your parents."

"They're not here," said the girl.

The third child, a little girl, pushed a way to the front step and eyed me curiously. "She's all snowy," she said. "Poor thing!"

I tried to smile at them but my face was frozen so that my lips moved slowly. "I won't hurt you," I said.

The girl said, "We'll talk it over. Wait there a minute."

The door closed and I thought I would faint with exhaustion. But that would alarm them and then they might lock me out. I willed myself to stay upright.

When the door opened the girl said, "We're not supposed to talk to strangers and we shouldn't ask you in but we can't leave you there on a night like this."

Ten minutes later I was sitting in a big, comfortable chair, wrapped in a blanket and the girl was feeding me with soup. I had learned their names and something about them.

The older girl was called Alison and she was twelve. The boy, her brother, was Charlie and he was nine. The younger girl was Stephanie and she was seven.

Their parents had gone to visit friends in the next town and couldn't get home because of the snow.

Charlie was full of questions. Why are you wearing that funny dress? Where do you come from? Where are you going?

I answered as best I could. I did not want to lie but how could I tell them the truth?

Slowly I began to feel a little more human. "The soup is very good," I told Alison.

She said something that sounded like "Hines".

I didn't understand but was too sleepy to ask for an explanation. The room was very warm although I could not see a fire anywhere. There was a box in the corner of the room with a glass front over which strange images flickered. Perhaps that was the fire. Things were so different these days. Every year there was something else I did not understand.

Charlie said, "We all helped to cook supper but that was before you came. Alison let us choose and I had beef burgers."

Stephanie piped up earnestly. "I had fish fingers and Alison had scrambled eggs."

I said, "Fish don't have fingers, do they?" but for some reason they all groaned.

Charlie said, "Not that corney old joke again!"

Alison smiled at me. "Take no notice of him," she advised. "He thinks he's so smart!"

It was my turn to ask some questions. "Why aren't you in your night attire? It's nearly midnight."

They exchanged sheepish glances.

Stephanie said, "Alison said we needn't."

Alison explained. "We feel a bit safer in our daytime clothes. It's a bit creepy in this cottage without Mum and Dad."

"Creepy?" I asked nervously. "How do you mean?"

"Well, it's next to the church and we can see all

the gravestones from the bedroom window. We did go to bed but then we all felt a bit scared so I said we should get up and get dressed again. We were watching an old movie on the telly just to pass the time. To take our minds off the church-yard and everything."

I felt the familiar pang of disappointment. People always knew. Someone always told them.

"What's creepy about a churchyard?" I asked. They looked at each other uneasily.

Alison said, "The lady in the post office says it's haunted and that the ghost wanders the village. We don't believe in ghosts – at least, I don't think so – but it is a bit scary. Do you believe in them?"

I did not know how to answer so I remained silent, pretending to consider the question.

Charlie said, "There's safety in numbers and now there's four of us. That should be enough."

I nodded but I was sick at heart. It was the same every year. I looked forward to the win-ter, hoping for deep snow, but then the rumours started again. If only they would forget me.

Alison said, "You look terribly tired. You could have a sleep if you wanted to. There's a bed made up in the spare room."

I accepted the offer willingly. The truth was I was afraid to talk further. I knew that they would eventually tell me about the girl who had died; the girl whose ghost haunted the village.

I did not want to hear it. I knew all about the unfortunate girl. She had lost her way in a snow blizzard and frozen to death less than a hundred metres from her own front door. I fell on to the bed and was asleep instantly.

Later I woke up and went downstairs. The three children had fallen asleep in the chairs and I tiptoed past them to the front door.

I turned briefly and whispered, "Goodbye!"

I was trudging away through the snow when the door opened again and Alison called after me: "Why are you going? You don't have to. Don't you want any breakfast?"

Charlie called, "It's beans on toast! You know! Beans means Heinz!" Then he laughed.

I longed with all my heart to go back but it would soon be daylight. I went on without a backward glance.

Suddenly I heard Alison cry out in shock. "Oh Charlie! Look!" she cried in a shaky voice. "That girl! She hasn't left any footprints in the snow!"

I sighed and struggled on through the snow which came up to my knees. Around me the sun glinted on a white wonderland. It looked so beautiful. So innocent.

But I knew better. I knew it was a killer.

THE PICTURE

The Picture

Ada Smith came into the lounge and stared in disbelief. "Well look at that!" she exclaimed. She waddled over to the fireplace and stared at the picture which hung at a crazy angle on the wall. May, her sister, followed her into the room.

"I hung that as straight as a die!" Ada told her. "Someone's been meddling with it." She looked round the room as though expecting the culprit to appear from behind the sofa.

May moved closer as her sister straightened the picture. "Whatever made you buy such a gloomy thing?" she asked. "Gives me the shivers just to look at it."

Both women regarded it critically for a moment. It was an oil painting showing the execution of a nobleman. He knelt beside the guillotine in his beautiful velvet suit and waited for the blade to fall.

May frowned. "Not exactly jolly, is it?" she demanded, not expecting an answer.

Her sister said sharply, "It's not meant to be jolly. It's meant to be dramatic. Mr Gray ex-

explained it all to me. It's about the French Revolution. Lots of people had their heads chopped off by the guillotine. I thought it was so lifelike. Just look at the expression in the man's eyes. Mr Gray said I'd got a bargain at five pounds."

"Is that all it was?" May was impressed. "Well, I suppose it was cheap. Mr Gray's usually a bit on the pricey side. I went in there Monday to ask about a little china dog. Twelve pounds, he wanted for it. Twelve!" She shook her head indignantly. "I thought he seemed very abrupt with me. Not his usual cheery self." She stared at the painting. "No, I don't care for it much. I wouldn't have it in my house. I tell you straight." She shuddered and said, "Let's go into the kitchen where we won't see it. It's giving me the creeps."

The following morning when Ada went into the lounge again she was shocked to find the picture at the same crazy angle as before.

"Well I'll be blowed!" she exclaimed.

Nobody had been into the room since she and May had left it the day before yet the picture had been moved.

She moved towards it, her face puzzled, and lifted it from the hook. Taking it to the window she examined it carefully. "Pictures don't move themselves," she said wonderingly. "So what's going on?"

At that moment the front door bell rang and she hurried to answer it. The vicar stood on the doorstep, smiling his usual gentle smile. "Ah Mrs Smith!" he said. "You've obviously guessed the reason for my visit. Is that picture for the jumble sale?"

Ada glanced at the picture which she carried under her arm. "Certainly not!" she told him with a laugh. "I've only just bought it. No, I've looked out some old books and a few ornaments for the sale."

She led the way into the kitchen and gave him a carrier bag which bulged with jumble. Then she showed him the picture. "My sister doesn't like it," she told him. "What do you think of it?"

To her surprise he seemed very interested in it and examined it closely.

"I can't make out the signature of the artist," he said. "But I'm sure I've seen it somewhere before. Or else something similar. I suppose it is rather gloomy for some tastes."

Ada explained that it kept going crooked. "So I'm going to try it in my bedroom," she said. "I wondered if it was the vibration that makes it move. The lounge faces on to the street, you see, and all these juggernaut things keep going past. My bedroom is at the back so it might be better there."

When he had gone she took the picture into her bedroom and hung it opposite the bed.

Her sister called in later that evening with some sad news.

"Poor Mr Gray's been taken to hospital," she told Ada. "Collapsed in a faint and had to be taken to hospital by ambulance. They don't know what it is, poor man. That's the worrying thing about it. They're calling it a mystery illness."

Ada stared. "Now I remember he was looking very pale when I bought the picture from him. He seemed very nervous. Poor man. I'll have to send him a 'Get well' card."

She made a cup of tea and they chatted for a while but Ada was quite pleased to see her sister go. Her own head was beginning to ache and she felt rather strange.

She went to the bedroom to lie down for half an hour – and had another shock. The picture was gone from the wall and even the nail was missing.

"Oh my Lord!" she whispered. "I don't like this at all."

Fearfully she looked around her – and saw something which made her cry out with shock. The picture now hung immediately over her bed!

"Oo-er!" she said and sat down heavily on the nearest chair. She tried to think of a logical explanation of what had happened. Either she had put it there herself without knowing what she was doing or someone (or some *thing*) had moved it for her. She shook her head violently as she considered this last possibility.

"It must have been me," she told herself firmly. "Perhaps I went into a bit of a trance – or maybe I'm getting very forgetful. Nobody else has been in the house and a picture couldn't move itself."

Trying not to let it worry her she left the picture where it was but decided not to have a sleep. She went back to the kitchen and made another cup of tea.

She was sipping it thoughtfully when the phone rang. It was May with bad news. Mr Gray was in intensive care and was not expected to survive the night. "And they still don't know what's causing it," she told Ada. The two sisters had known Mr Gray for more than twenty years and both were saddened by the news. Ada was so upset that she quite forgot to tell her sister about the picture.

That night she went to bed with a very bad headache and a sharp pain in her neck. Later she woke in a fright and sat bolt upright in bed. At once she sensed that someone was in the room! She was sure of it.

"Who's there?" she cried in a trembling voice.

She switched on the bedside lamp – and saw that the room was empty.

"But something woke me!" she cried. "Something happened. Someone was here!"

Normally she slept heavily and only woke when the alarm clock sounded. She knew that something had disturbed her sleep – but what.

Suddenly she heard a strange sound. It was very far off but she recognized the swish of steel . . .

It was followed by a thud and then a clamour of excited voices which grew to a terrifying roar of triumph.

"The sound of the guillotine!" she whispered. "But that's impossible. The French Revolution was two hundred years ago!"

Hardly knowing what to expect she turned to look at the picture but to her relief the nobleman still knelt beside the guillotine - and his head still rested on his shoulders. Her relief did not last long, however. The picture began to tremble and then it sprang from the wall as though seized by unseen hands. It hovered for a moment in the air and then it twisted so violently that the frame split apart and the canvas was torn in half.

With a squeal of fear Ada slid from the bed and ran for the door. Her one idea was to get out of the room while she was still in one piece. A very powerful spirit was obviously at work in the room; a spirit strong enough to destroy the picture. She did not want to be its next victim!

She was halfway to the bedroom door when the

damaged picture hurtled across the room and out through the door, narrowly missing her head. As Ada screamed, the picture smashed itself against the landing wall and rolled crazily down the stairs. There, it lay motionless, ruined beyond repair.

"Heaven preserve us!" she whispered shakily, hoping against hope that the worst was over.

Ada's heart was beating so hard she could hardly draw breath.

"Oh someone help me!" she cried. But who could she turn to? May would be no use for she would be as frightened as Ada was.

She thought suddenly of the vicar. A man of God ought to know how to deal with evil spirits.

She ran into the kitchen and dialled his number with trembling fingers. As she waited for him to answer she glanced at the clock. Midnight. A dangerous hour, she thought ruefully.

It seemed an age before the vicar picked up the phone. When she explained what was happening he promised to come round right away and bring a crucifix.

While she waited she put on her dressing gown and took the curlers out of her hair.

When she heard his knock at the front door, however, she received another shock. The picture was nowhere to be seen.

With a trembling finger Ada pointed to the foot of the stairs. "But it was there!" she cried, pointing. "All torn and twisted. I didn't imagine it. It was there, I tell you!"

The vicar shook his head. "I don't doubt your word," he told her. "To tell you the truth I think you have had a very lucky escape. I have had doubts about the picture ever since I first saw it. I decided to try and find out the name of the artist. I did a bit of reading in the library this morning and —"

He paused and Ada said, "Go on! I might as well hear it all."

"Well, it seems it was painted by a young Frenchman, the day after his father was executed. Two days later they arrested him and he met the same fate as his father."

Ada sat down on the edge of the bed. "So what was it exactly?" she asked. "His ghost?"

The vicar shrugged. "A vengeful spirit, certainly. Maybe the malevolent ghost of the young Frenchman — or his father. We shall probably never know. Some things are beyond the understanding of man."

Suddenly Ada's eyes widened as a new thought struck her. "Do you think the ghost was trying to harm poor Mr Gray before I bought the picture? Was the vengeful ghost trying to make Mr Gray ill? I began to feel ill. It could have been the picture. Oo-er!"

"Anything's possible," he said.

"But if the picture's gone now – ?" She left the sentence unfinished.

The vicar smiled. "I should think you are safe now," he agreed. "As for poor Mr Gray – we shall have to wait and see."

The following day Ada called in on her sister to tell her about the previous night's adventure. Before she could open her mouth, however, May had some news of her own.

"It's Mr Gray," she said with a broad smile. "He's not going to die after all. It seems that quite unexpectedly he made a turn for the better and – "

It was Ada's turn to smile. "Let me guess," she said. "His about-turn came at exactly twelve o'clock last night!"

May stared at her in amazement. "Well, it's true," she said "But how did you know?"

"It's a long story," said Ada "but if you put the kettle on for a cup of tea I'll tell you all about it!"

THE
CAROL SINGERS

The Carol Singers

The wind howled around the little church, whistling in at the broken window and out through the empty belfry. It stood amongst flat fields and brooding dykes, dilapidated, forgotten.

The tiny churchyard was overgrown and full of weeds and the once neat path was green with moss. One of the church windows had been broken in a storm and was now boarded up.

It was dusk and an owl hooted eerily in the branches of the sycamore while small nocturnal creatures scuttled about among the dry leaves that lay everywhere.

Inside the church three men were deep in conversation. One of them was Edmund, a not very successful highwayman. He had been killed by a blunderbuss towards the end of the eighteenth century. His face was gaunt with deepset eyes and his manner was gloomy.

By contrast, Oliver was a handsome man, a little tubby perhaps, but cheerful. He had once been a promising artist until his talent led him astray. He became a skilful forger of paper money but the law caught up with him and hanged him.

Roland, the youngest, was fond of telling people that he was the youngest son of a belted earl. He was fair with a receding chin and had not lived beyond the age of eighteen. He had run away to sea and had been drowned sailing round the Horn.

Oliver said, "Well, are we or aren't we?"

Edmund shrugged his thin shoulders. "Is it worth it? Does anybody really care?" he said.

Roland looked at his friends with dismay. "Of course they care! People expect it," he reminded them. "They talk about us for miles around. We can't let them down. It wouldn't be Christmas in Braybury without our carol singing."

Edmund was unconvinced. "But now we're only three. It was so much better when there were four of us. We were balanced. If only Sam was still with us. He wasn't the best baritone in the world, I grant you that, but he was quite nifty with the squeeze-box."

They were all silent, lamenting the recent departure of their erstwhile companion. Sam had lived in the seventeenth century. He had been a street-seller of cooked meats until the unfortunate business with the tainted mutton. Seven people had died of food poisoning, including Sam.

Roland said, "Well, the way I see it three is better than none. We'll just have to sing louder than ever. My vote is that we go ahead. I've remembered a little French carol I used to know. I thought we might include it. Add a little class to the entertainment. Lift it from the mundane." He ducked as a bat flew past them and out through the side door which hung open on sagging hinges.

Oliver looked doubtful. "I don't know about French," he murmured.

Edmund also hesitated. "Three's neither here nor there," he said. "It won't sound right. I vote we forget it."

Roland's mouth tightened. Trust Edmund to give in at the first hurdle. It was typical of the man. But what could you expect from a highwayman? They were utterly selfish. Loyal to no one but themselves. Now Sam had been a better man altogether. Sam knew the value of friendship. It was a pity he had gone but his had been one of the oldest graves in the churchyard and one of the first to go.

They were widening the road and had taken over part of the disused churchyard. All the oldest graves had been bulldozed. Roland wondered how long it would be before his own corner of the churchyard would be needed for the living.

With an effort he brought his thoughts back to the matter in hand. Would they or would they not go carol singing this coming Christmas?

"I could practise the squeeze-box," he offered,

"if one of you will carry the lantern. There's still more than a week to go. I won't be as good as Sam but I'll do my best. I can – " He stopped in mid sentence. Muffled voices were coming from outside the church and all three stiffened in amazement. It was a rare occasion when anyone dared to walk through the haunted churchyard.

Roland put a finger to his lips and they all glided quickly through the church wall to discover the identity of the intruders.

Two men were making their way unsteadily along the overgrown path. They had their arms draped around each other to keep themselves upright and both were the worse for drink. One was the local postman who had been celebrating his sixtieth birthday. The other was a younger man who worked as a gardener.

The three ghosts watched as the two drunks fell over a low gravestone and ended up on the ground, giggling and waving their legs in the air.

Roland regarded them with disgust. "Pathetic!" he said. "Whatever do they look like!" He did not really expect an answer.

Edmund tutted. "And this is hallowed ground," he said.

Suddenly the postman sat up and stared round him. "Oh Lordy!" he said. "We're in the churchyard! There be ghosts here!"

"Ghosts my eye!" said the gardener. "I've never seen no ghosts. Hic! Not nowhere."

The postman stuggled to stand up, clutching on to the gravestone to steady himself. "Haven't you heard of them ghostly carol singers?" he demanded. "They walk round the churchyard on Christmas Eve and one of them carries a lantern and one plays an accordian. There's four of them. You can see right through them. My aunt saw them once. Wailing and carrying on they was. Frightened the living daylights out of her!"

Roland said indignantly, "Wailing? Damned cheek!"

Edmund said, "I told you they don't appreciate us. All that practising and learning words for nothing."

The postman was trying to pull the gardener to his feet. "We'd best get out of here" he said. "Case they get us!"

"Who's that then?" asked the gardener.

"The ghosts, stupid!" He looked round fearfully.

The gardener said rashly, "I tell you I'm not scared of a few ghosties! Carol singing indeed. Hic! I can sing as well as any of them." He staggered to his feet, threw out his arms and began to sing. "Good King Wenceslas looked out, On the feast of – "

"Hush!" cried the postman. "They might hear

you!" He stared round the apparently deserted churchyard.

"Good thing if they do!" cried the gardener. He tried to remember which carol he was singing, failed and went on to another. "We three kings of Orient are. Bearing gifts we – Hic! – traverse afar. . ."

Roland said slowly, "Well I never! He's a baritone!"

Edmund smiled. "A good one, too."

Oliver looked at Roland and Roland looked at Edmund. Soon they were all smiling.

"Another baritone!" said Oliver. "Are you two thinking what I'm thinking?"

While they were talking the gardener had tripped over a length of trailing ivy. He now lay in a patch of nettles with his eyes shut while he sang two verses of "Away in a manger."

Oliver was impressed. "He even sounds good lying down!" he said.

Without further ado he stepped forward and towered over the prostrate gardener. Gradually he resumed his human shape. He was half-transparent in the best ghostly tradition but his silk breeches and ruffled shirt looked well on him.

He coughed and the gardener opened his eyes. He took one look at him and the carol died on his lips. "L-l-look!" he quavered.

Edmund, smiling faintly, joined his friend and he, too, began to materialize. He was dressed in his highwayman's coat, knee boots and a tricorne hat.

The gardener scrambled to his knees.

"What's up with you?" cried the postman, who could see nothing unusual.

"Gh-gh-ghosts!" cried the gardener. He wanted to run away but his legs were like jelly.

Roland appeared next, every inch a sailor in his pale blue breeches, striped jersey and bare feet.

The gardener let out a screech of terror. "It's th-th-them!" he stammered.

He began to run, hiccuping, lurching and stumbling around the tip-tilted gravestones. His one idea was to find the church gate and escape on to the newly widened road. Once he was outside the churchyard he knew he would be safe for no one had ever seen the ghostly carol singers beyond the churchyard wall. Fear sharpened the gardener's wits and he dodged this way and that but the three ghosts were too clever for him. One of them was always just ahead of him and whenever he turned to escape that one he would find himself confronted by another. His terror grew as he rushed wildly in all directions. The postman tried to reason with him in vain and then suddenly – it happened!

The gardener gave a strangled cry and clutched

his throat. He doubled up and fell to his knees, gasping and choking. The postman, sobered by the shocking events, ran to him.

"Are you all right?" he asked.

The gardener's eyes rolled in his head. He tried to say that "No, he was not all right! Hic! Did he look all right?!" All he could manage, however, was a terrible croak and then he plunged forward and lay still, his face cushioned by a convenient patch of dock leaves.

He was dead.

Oliver said, "Oh well done, chaps!"

Edmund grinned wickedly. "So now we are four again!" he said.

Oliver shook hands with Edmund and Edmund shook hands with Roland. They stared with delight at the prone figure on the ground before them.

Edmund said, "Poor fellow. Still, it was in a good cause. We do need another baritone."

Roland nodded. "He knows the words, too. That's a great help."

They were still congratulating themselves when Edmund happened to glance at the postman. He had staggered away to the church door and was leaning against it. Now he began to slip downwards.

"Oh no!" muttered Edmund. "Not him, too!"

They rushed over to investigate and sure

enough the postman was also dead. The death of his friend in such bizarre circumstances had been too much for his sixty-year-old heart.

Edmund, Oliver and Roland regarded him without enthusiasm.

"Now why did he have to do that?" Roland asked crossly. He sighed heavily. "Some people just can't see when they're not wanted."

"Perhaps he can sing too," said Oliver, trying to look on the bright side.

Edmund shook his head. "Even if he can we don't want him. We've got two tenors and two baritones. Anyone else will unbalance us again."

They stared down at him for a long minute and then Roland brightened a little. "Never mind," he said. "He can carry the lantern."

ALL
HALLOWS EVE

All Hallows Eve

Tim and Sally had decided to give a hallowe'en party. They would hold it in the barn and it would be very scary.

"No pussy-footing about!" said Tim. "We'll tell anyone who comes that it's going to be very frightening and if they don't want to be frightened they needn't come."

Sally agreed. "But what can we do to frighten them?" she asked. "Whatever we do they'll know it's only us."

"I've thought of that," he told her. "We'll make up a ghostly ordeal and they must each come into the barn and suffer it alone. No coming in pairs so they can giggle and mess about. One at a time."

After much heated discussion they finally worked out a plan. The guests would wait outside the barn and would take it in turns to enter. As soon as they came through the door the candle would be blown out and a tape would begin to play ghostly laughter. Then, before they could become accustomed to the darkness a cloth would be dropped over them from above. Sally would then take hold of one of their hands and say, "Come. Wash your hands in vampire's blood!" And she would plunge their hands into a bowl of warm water. In the darkness their imagination would do the rest.

"It sounds marvellous, so far," said Sally with a grin. "I'm glad I'm in on it. I'd hate to be one of the victims!"

The tape would then go on again – a loud scream followed by a lot of groaning – and the "heart of a vampire" would be placed in the victim's hands. This would be a balloon half-filled with water.

"They'll believe anything we tell them," crowed Tim, "as long as the atmosphere's right." His eyes shone with excitement as he warmed to his theme. "We'll dress up a dummy and lay it out on a table and pretend it's a human sacrifice – "

Sally pulled a face. "I don't like that idea," she said. "Don't let's get too horrid. It's only meant to be a bit of fun."

"Oh don't be such a baby!" Tim told her scornfully. "Don't you understand, they'll want to be frightened. That's the whole point of Hallowe'en. Ghosties and things that go bump in the night! We'll put a dagger into their hand and say– "

"A dagger? Are you mad?" Sally was getting a little nervous.

"A plastic dagger, silly! Then we tell them to stab the human sacrifice. They'll know it's not a real person."

"I still don't like it."

"You're chicken!"

"I'm not! It's just that I don't think we should scare them too much," she protested. "You wouldn't like it if you were the victim."

"I wouldn't mind because I wouldn't be scared," Tim told her loftily. "Look, either stay and co-operate or give up the idea of helping and become one of the victims."

Sally hesitated. She really did not fancy that at all so after a little thought she was forced to give in.

They went ahead with the preparations and even Sally had to admit that the ghostly tape they made sounded very convincing. The "human sacrifice" was made out of clothes stuffed with straw. At the end of each "ordeal" the victim would make his or her way out through a second door at the back of the barn, through six plastic spiders hung on threads!

When all was ready, four of their friends were invited to the Hallowe'en festivities. They all accepted with great enthusiasm.

On the appointed day they all met in the farmyard

as arranged, at half-past seven. Each one wore fancy dress and carried a candle.

Sally was a witch complete with tall, pointed hat. Tim was a werewolf with hairy hands and fangs. Mary was dressed as a ghost in an old sheet and Stuart came as a sorcerer in a star spangled cloak. Anna was a bat with black wings made from an old curtain and long black fingernails and Dennis was a devil with horns and a black tail.

In the flickering gleam of the candles they looked a hideous group and they spent the first ten minutes admiring each other's costumes.

"Now we start," said Sally. "First we shall offer you a glass of red poison and a handful of rabbits' bones!"

They all shrieked with horror and pretended not to notice that the "poison" was in fact Ribena and that the "rabbits' bones" looked remarkably like Twiglets! Eaten by the light of the candles anything seemed possible.

At last the dread moment arrived – the ordeals were about to begin! Sally and Tim retired to the barn and called in the first victim.

The devil appeared in the doorway and the ghostly laughter began. Dennis began to speak but only got as far as "Now, don't you – " before the cloth dropped over his head and he gave a shriek of alarm.

Sally took hold of his hand and, in a disguised

voice, said, "Come. Wash your hands in the blood of a vampire!" She guided Dennis's hands into the bowl of warm water and felt him shudder.

The rest of the ordeal went according to plan and when Dennis finally escaped into the farmyard again they listened with satisfaction as he told the others how awful it had been.

"So far, so good!" said Tim, but before Sally could answer the next willing victim came in. On went the ghostly laughter and down came the cloth. . .

Mary, the ghost, was last in and that's when things began to go wrong. Just as she entered the barn Sally reached out to switch on the tape but before she could do so a horrible ghostly cackle filled the barn. It grew louder and louder until it was almost unbearable and they were all forced to put their fingers in their ears.

"Turn it down, you idiot!" shouted Tim.

"It's not me!" Sally shouted back. "I mean it's not the tape! I don't know what it is!"

As suddenly as it had started the laughter stopped and the sudden silence was even more terrifying.

At the top of the ladder Tim prepared to drop the cloth but at that very moment something fell over his own head. Half-suffocated he overbalanced and with a muffled cry he fell off the ladder. Fortunately he landed on the straw but as he sprawled on his back something cold and horribly slimy wriggled across his face. He thrust it away with a shudder of distaste and then he became aware of a dense, pervasive fog – a mixture of rotting weed and foul, dank air which filled his mouth and nose. It smelt of decay and death and Tim began to cough and choke.

His thoughts raced as he made an effort to control his terror. Somebody was trying to turn the tables and frighten him! Probably Sally, he thought angrily.

"You wait!" he called but his voice shook, betraying his fear.

He struggled furiously to his feet and as he did so a sound high in the rafters of the barn made him look up. There he saw a pale, shimmering shape with red smouldering eyes.

He stared up at it doubtfully, his heart thumping wildly. That could never be Sally! Not right up there!

He was seized by an overwhelming desire to be out of the barn and back among his friends. But where were the two girls?

"Sally!" he called. "Mary! Where are you? I'm getting out of here!"

There was no answer. He glanced round uneasily. A hand on his arm made him jump.

"For heaven's sake!" he cried shakily. "You scared me half to death!"

"That's the idea, isn't it?" The voice was deep and husky, almost gravelly. It did not sound like Sally or Mary.

"Look," Tim began. "I've had enough of this. Let's call it all off and – " A face appeared before him and he let out a yell of pure terror. It was a grinning skull, lit from within, so that it glowed eerily.

Another face appeared. This one was misshapen and ugly. The eyes bulged and the lips were twisted into a hateful grin. It seemed to be made of melting wax for the features moved and sagged. It was horribly real.

For a moment he thought he was going to faint but then, with a tremendous effort he forced himself to stay calm. Of course it was Mary and Sally. It must be! It was very clever, he admitted that, but maybe he could still beat them. He would lock them in the barn.

He made a wild dash to the far door and, brushing aside the spiders, turned the key in the lock. Then, with the key in his hand, he ran back to the main door and pulled it open. He gave a last glance back inside the barn. The two hideous faces watched him go.

He dashed outside and pulled the door closed behind him. Then he bolted it. Let them stew in there for a bit, he thought. That would teach them to play tricks on him!

The others crowded round eagerly.

"Tim!" cried Dennis. "That was fantastic! Really super!"

Tim drew a deep breath. He must speak normally. He must never let them know how terrified he had been. "Glad you enjoyed it!" he said.

"I'm sorry I ran like that," said Mary. "That laughter was so frightening. My courage failed me."

Tim's heart skipped a beat. Mary was supposed to be shut in the barn with Sally! How on earth had she got out?

Sally said shakily, "That wasn't us. Truly it wasn't. Was it, Mary?"

Tim turned to her in growing horror. If neither of the girls were locked in the barn then –

Mary laughed. "I'm sorry I missed it, Tim, but Sally and I just fled!" She slipped an arm through Sally's. "But don't let's talk about it any more. I'm starving! All that terror has given me an appetite!"

Tim leaned back weakly against the side of the barn.

Sally said, "Mum's laid out some food for us in the kitchen. Come on." And she led them all into the house.

All except Tim. He watched them go in shocked silence while the hair on the back of his neck rose.

If Sally and Mary had run from the barn when the loud laughter started they were not responsible for the skull or the melting face – or any of it! The key of the far door was in his pocket and the main door was bolted on the outside and Sally and Mary were outside the barn. "Then who – or what – have I locked in the barn?" he whispered.

For a moment he was tempted to find out and he put out a trembling hand to pull back the bolt on the barn door. Then he remembered what he had seen and felt and suddenly knew that he dare not go back.

Whatever was in the barn would remain a mystery.

He drew a deep breath of fresh air into his lungs and waited for his legs to stop trembling. Then he followed the others into the house.

PIANO PRACTICE

Piano Practice

Phil rolled over on to his back and glared at the ancient upright piano that took up so much space in his room. It had belonged to his grandmother many years ago and when she died she left it to him in her will. All because he had told her that he wanted to be a concert pianist! He groaned aloud. He should have kept his big mouth shut, he told himself irritably. The keyboard was out of sight. He had locked the lid. That way he would not be tempted.

His mother called up the stairs. "Phil! Get on with your practice!" She had a friend coming round later. Someone she had met at the library.

He did not answer. He knew the exam was less than a week away but he also knew he could not pass it. Grade Six was impossibly hard. He simply could not do it. No amount of practice would make it possible.

Downstairs the phone shrilled and he heard his mother answer it. Then she called up the stairs again. "It's for you, Phil. It's Simon."

He leaped from the bed and rushed downstairs.

"Phil? It's Simon. About tonight. Are you coming?"

"Course I am!" said Phil.

Simon, Tim and Alec were all going to the local disco and Tim was borrowing his father's car. Phil wasn't all that keen on the disco but all of his schoolfriends would be there and if he didn't go they would rag him unmercifully on Monday morning.

"I'll be there," he said.

"We'll pick you up at eight."

"Fine."

But was it fine, he wondered, as he replaced the receiver? All that noise and the darkness and so many people smoking. The smoke always made him cough, the music almost deafened him and the fancy strobe lighting gave him a headache. Still, the others seemed to like it.

His mother appeared at the door of the lounge. "Are you going out?" she asked. Her question held an unspoken accusation. He ought to be practising for the exam. That was what she was really saying.

"I'm going to the disco. They'll pick me up at eight," he told her and pretended not to see her look of disappointment. Damn Grandma and her blasted piano!

He went upstairs, slowly, his thoughts confused. His grandmother had left him the piano, enough money for lessons and a bit extra to get it tuned regularly. It had a sweet tone, he would admit that. For such an old piano it was surprisingly mellow. He loved the way it sounded; loved the power of his fingers as they swept across the keyboard, searching out the right notes, creating something beautiful. He loved the sheet music from which he played – anything from Rachmaninoff to Scott Joplin! It was true, he confessed, that he did love the piano and he had wanted, quite desperately, to be a concert pianist.

But that was before he started the lessons and realized what hard work it was. Not to mention the amount of time he was forced to devote to it. Not to mention his friends who thought he was mad to spend his evenings shut up in his room.

This last exam was the crucial one. He must pass it if he was to go any further with his music. The Guildhall School of Music! That had been his goal for so many years and he was almost there.

Back in his room he stood in front of the piano and suddenly he frowned. Funny! The lid was open now and yet he was certain he had left it locked.

"I must be cracking up!" he grinned and before he knew what he was doing he had tapped out the melody of *D'you ken John Peel*.

Suddenly he was overcome with longing to sit down on the stool and play it properly. "I can't!" he whispered.

How could he tell his classmates that he would rather play the piano than join them at the disco or the football field or wherever they happened to be?

He glanced at the clock and saw that he had just over half an hour to get ready. He rushed to the bathroom and gave himself a quick wash – no time for a bath.

He wondered who would be at the disco. Probably that awful Susan that Tim liked and the Barnet sisters with their funny teeth and Meg Butler making horrible jokes that he never could understand (although he always laughed!).

He pulled a clean shirt from the drawer and buttoned it without enthusiasm. His fingers were itching to play something – anything! He did not always use a score. He could improvise. His father would name a tune and Phil would play it. Just like that.

He ran a comb through his hair and pulled a face at himself in the mirror. Now if Jenny Seaton was going to be at the disco that would be different. His face glowed at the thought of her. But her parents were very strict and she was never allowed to go. He thought of her large dark eyes and sweet round face. She was not exactly pretty but there was something about her – he did not quite know what.

The clock said eight o'clock and he sat on the edge of the bed, trying to ignore the piano and the overpowering urge he had to play it.

Five past eight.

Ten past.

He walked to the piano and looked with affection at the worn ivories, yellow now with age. His grandmother had been a music teacher before arthritis made her give it up. She had encouraged him as a very young boy, playing scraps of music, sliding her gnarled old hands over the keys as though she loved each one. He sat down and allowed his hands to rest on the keys, imagining his grandmother's voice. . .

Suddenly he could smell her perfume. For special occasions she had always worn "Evening in Paris". He smiled and turned, almost expecting to see her small, dumpy figure in the brown skirt and fawn jumper which she always wore. She had plenty of other clothes, he knew, but they were her favourites.

Twenty past eight! What had happened to his friends?

He began to play *Greensleeves*, one of her

favourite pieces. He had not played for almost three weeks but his hands had lost none of their cunning. He smiled as his fingers caressed the notes, effortlessly, with deep satisfaction.

After that he played several pieces from *Die Schöne Müllerin* by Schubert and then something by Chopin which he had always enjoyed playing. Then he remembered the Bach prelude he had performed at the school concert and played that. He didn't need to look for the music, he knew them by heart. They were like old friends.

Friends!

He stopped in mid phrase, his fingers poised over the keys. What on earth had happened to his friends? He glanced at the clock and saw that it was five to nine but somehow he no longer cared. He went on playing as if his life depended on it, like a thirsty man drinking water.

At wenty past nine his mother called up the stairs and he stopped reluctantly.

"Jenny Seaton's here," she told him. "She's been listening to you play. I thought perhaps you'd let her come up and watch you practise."

His heart leaped with excitement. But what was Jenny Seaton doing here? Cautiously he went half-way down the stairs.

His mother was looking very cheerful, he thought. "I told you I had a friend coming round," she explained. "It was Mary Seaton. Jenny came with her."

"I didn't know you knew Mrs Seaton," he mumbled.

His mother laughed. "I don't have to tell you everything, Phil," she said. "We met at the library last week."

Jenny appeared behind her and at the sight of her Phil's pulse rate soared!

"I love Chopin," she said shyly. "I'd love to listen but I won't if it will put you off."

"No," he stammered. "Come on up."

The next hour passed in a whirl. It seemed that Jenny adored music. She and her mother went to the ballet in London and once she had gone to Covent Garden to the Royal Opera House to see the opera *Carmen*.

She was terribly impressed with his skill at the piano and the fact that he was going in for Grade 6. She told him that she and her mother were going to get tickets for a concert at the Festival Hall and asked him if he wanted to join them. Before she left he played her favourite tune - *The Sting* by Scott Joplin and she said she'd had a marvellous time.

She'd had a marvellous time! So had Phil!

The next morning he met up with Tim on the school bus and asked him what had happened.

"What about?" said Tim, puzzled.

"The disco, you nut!" said Phil. "You were going to pick me up."

Tim stared at him. "But you changed your mind. You decided to practise for the exam. Your grandma told us. It was OK."

It was Phil's turn to stare. "My – my grandma?" he stammered. "But she's been – " She had been dead four years but he could not say it.

"She met us at the gate and said you'd changed your mind. She said she was your grandma."

Phil swallowed hard. "What was she like?" he asked.

"A bit tubby. Small. She had on a dark skirt and – "

"Yes," said Phil quickly. "That was her." He sat back feeling very peculiar.

Tim looked at him in surprise. "Are you OK?" he asked. "You've gone all pale and interesting!"

"I'm all right."

His grandmother's ghost had waited at the gate to tell his friends he was not going to the disco! And because of her he had stayed in and had a wonderful evening – and he and Jenny were going to a concert together!

His throat felt very tight and he felt a prickle of tears at his eyelids. "Thanks, Gran!" he thought. "I really love you. And I'll pass that exam if it's the last thing I do!"

As the bus pulled up in the school playground Phil felt a sudden surge of confidence. Of course he could go to the Guildhall of Music! Of course he could be a concert pianist! With a grandmother like his, how could he fail?

THE
HAUNTED TRACK

The Haunted Track

Alex stood on the weed covered track and stared up and then down the line. Then he pointed with his walking stick. "That's the way back to Rye," he told his companion, "and that's the way to Camber. This was the station. We've got a photograph of my grandmother sitting on a seat with the trellis fence behind her. The station must have been about here – " he pointed towards a large clump of ferns.

Susan nodded and glanced down at the rotting remains of the wooden sleepers. The metal rails had long since been removed for scrap. "It's a very narrow track," she said. "It must have been a very small tram."

"It was called a tramway but actually it was a train," he corrected her. "A three foot gauge steam train. It used to stop right here where we're standing and all the golfers used to get off. Golf Links Station, it was called." He pointed again. "The golf course is somewhere over there."

Susan said, "But where's the sea? I thought you said we were going to the beach?"

"We are," he told her, "but we have to walk a bit further. The next stop was Camber Sands and that's where we're going to swim."

Susan looked around. "Did your grandmother come here for her holidays, then?"

"No, of course not. I thought I told you. Her father was one of the drivers so she used to get free rides whenever there was room on the train. According to Mum my grandmother loved this old tramway and sometimes used to play truant from school."

"Just so she could ride on the train, you mean?"

He nodded, laughing.

"Do you remember your grandmother?" Susan asked.

Alex shook his head. "She died while my mother was still a girl."

"What did she die of?" asked Susan curiously.

"Mum will tell you some time," he said. "She tells it better than I do. Come on – I'll race you to that tree. Ready, steady, go!"

As they set off along what was left of the weed covered track the young woman followed slowly behind them, a faint smile on her face. She liked the boy, and the girl seemed pleasant enough. They had stopped at the tree, out of breath from their race and she, too, waited. It woud never do to catch them up.

Glancing back at the station she saw Bill Hicks on the platform and he lifted his cap and waved to her. As she waved back she smiled. Poor Bill! That uniform never did fit him properly – sleeves too short and trousers too long! They used to tease him but he didn't mind. Easy going, that was Bill Hicks. . .

She walked on as soon as they did, holding her long skirt clear of the ground, stepping carefully in her best buttoned boots, ever mindful of the gleaming rails. Once she had been careless and had tripped and gone sprawling. Very undignified! She smiled at the memory. It would never do to fall today, she thought, wearing her new brown silk.

She wondered how old the boy was. Probably not more than fourteen. She had been courting at fifteen and married at seventeen. Today they waited until they were older. . .

Suddenly she saw the young girl trip and nearly fall but the boy caught her arm just in time and she heard them laugh. They hurried on and she followed, keeping her distance.

"So how did she die?" asked Susan as they ran into the water.

"I told you. I'll tell you some other time," said Alex.

"But why the mystery?"

"You'll understand when I tell you."

"Tell me now, you beast!" she cried but he ran laughing into deeper water and she plunged in after him.

The water was very warm and their corner of the beach was almost deserted. Suddenly Susan saw a woman standing at the water's edge. She wore a long brown dress and a straw hat with ribbons.

"Alex!" she hissed. "Look at that woman. She's wearing fancy dress."

"So she is," he answered. "I wonder if they're making a film. They often do film at Camber."

"You mean she's a film star?"

"I expect so." He looked around at the empty beach. "But where's the film crew? No cameras. No directors. No nothing."

Together they waded towards the shore.

"She's watching us," said Susan and she raised a hand in greeting and called, "Hullo!"

The woman appeared startled. She put a hand to her mouth, then, to their surprise, turned and began to run away, scrambling and stumbling across the sand.

Alex shouted, "Please come back! We didn't mean to startle you."

But the woman ran faster, glancing anxiously back over her shoulder as though she feared they would follow her.

"What's the matter with her?" said Alex, feeling strangely disappointed.

"What did I say?" asked Susan. "I only said 'Hullo'."

By this time the woman had disappeared over the sand dunes. Susan and Alex walked back up the beach and sat on their towels.

"Perhaps she's mad," said Susan.

"She didn't look mad," said Alex slowly. "In fact I keep thinking I know her. There was something familiar about her but I can't think what it was."

They talked about her for a few minutes and then dried themselves off and began to eat their sandwiches. A dog appeared as if by magic and they had a lot of fun, throwing sticks for it to chase and racing it along the beach. Their odd visitor was soon forgotten.

They were on their way back to Rye and had almost reached the remains of Golf Links Station when they saw her again.

This time she was walking along what was left of the old track. Her head was down and there was something agitated in the way she moved.

"What is the matter with her?" asked Susan.

Alex shook his head without replying.

Suddenly, to their astonishment, they heard the whistle of an engine and looking towards Rye saw the smoke of an approaching train.

They looked at each other in disbelief.

"But that's impossible!" gasped Alex. He pointed a trembling finger and Susan gasped with shock. A narrow gauge steam train was approaching along the non-existent track. Its paintwork was bright and its funnel belched clouds of white smoke!

Susan clutched Alex's arm, too frightened to utter a word as relentlessly the train came towards them.

"That woman!" cried Susan. "Can't she hear it? She's standing right in its path!"

The whistle blew again and at last the woman glanced up and saw the train. But she saw it too late.

The driver slammed on his brakes but nothing happened and the little train continued out of control. It jolted and rattled, faster and faster and they heard the woman scream as it struck her. As Alex and Susan watched horrified, her body was tossed to one side like a rag doll thrown by a careless child.

Still the train came on, rocking wildly from side to side – but now it came towards Alex and Susan. Paralysed with shock they made no move to save themselves but clung together, as though awaiting their fate.

The train, with a hideous clatter, raced towards them, reached them – and passed right through them!

As it did so they caught a glimpse of the driver's white face as he struggled desperately to bring the runaway train to a halt.

Then it had gone and the silence was terrifying.

"That poor woman," cried Susan. "We must help her. She might be still alive."

She took a few steps forward but to her surprise Alex held her back.

"She's dead," he said quietly. "She's been dead for a long time."

Susan stared at him. He was very pale and looked badly shaken. "What on earth do you mean?" she demanded. "Of course we must help her. You can't know she's dead without even seeing her."

"Do you see her?" he asked.

Susan turned to look and was too shocked to speak. There was no sign of the woman, dead or alive. Just grass and sand.

"But where – " she stammered. "What happened? She must be – "

"And the train," said Alex. "Can you see the train?"

Utterly bewildered Susan discovered that the train, too, had disappeared.

Alex said slowly, "I thought I'd seen her somewhere. It was in the old photograph album. That was my grandmother's ghost. She was run down by a train. She was standing on the track, expecting the train to stop at the station as usual. Her own father was driving it. Something went wrong and the brakes failed. She was killed. She left a little girl of four. That was my mother."

Susan sat down suddenly, her legs weak.

After a moment she said, "So that's why you wouldn't tell me what she died of. You knew this place was haunted!"

"I'd heard rumours but I wanted to find out for myself. Some people claim to have heard the train. Others say they have seen the woman."

He held out his hands and pulled her to her feet.

"It scared me half to death," she told him reproachfully.

"That's why she was following us," he said. "Because she knew me. Perhaps she wanted to make contact with the family again."

"I could have died of fright!" Susan told him. "Then you'd have had two ghosts to worry about!"

"I'm really sorry," he said. "It's all my fault. I should never have brought you here."

"It's OK," she told him. "You couldn't have guessed what would happen."

They started walking towards the town and halfway there Alex stopped.

"But I'm sort of glad we met her," he said. "If it's made her ghost any happier. Do you think it has?"

"I think it's quite likely," said Susan. And she slipped an arm round his waist and they walked back to Rye feeling strangely comforted.

THE DEEP ONE

The Deep One

The gaoler was a swarthy man with unkempt hair and ignorant ways. His name was Jake Wicket and he had no friend in all the world.

He treated the prisoners with a carelessness which amounted to cruelty. He often forgot to give them their meagre rations and rarely let them out of their cells for exercise. If any man dared to protest at this harsh treatment he was punished.

Sam Tyson was fourteen years old and had been locked up in the gaol for more than a year. His crime was stealing a loaf of bread for his sister's children to save them from starving. Sam had no idea when he would get out of the gaol. Some gave up all hope and died there.

But Sam was not easily defeated, being by nature an optimist, and he did his best to survive.

The other unfortunates nick-named him Smiler becaue he was always cheerful, but he had one enemy. That was Jake Wicket, the gaoler. He hated Sam becaue the boy refused to be cowed by his many unkindnesses.

One afternoon the five men crowded together in the small dungeon were playing cards to pass the time when the gaoler looked in through the bars in the door.

"Oy! You lot! Pack that up!" he cried, seeing that the men were managing to enjoy themselves. "You know the rules. No gambling! No profanities. No – "

"No food!" cried Sam recklessly, with a wink at his companions. "No exercise!"

Jake's hard eyes glittered. It was just the excuse he had been looking for. A chance to inflict some further punishment upon the young boy. "That's enough lip from you, you young cub!" he roared. "For that you'll get bread and water for a week!"

"A feast!" cried Sam, refusing to show any fear in the face of the man's rage.

Jake's mouth became a thin hard line. "And for that you'll spend the night on your own, in the Deep One! We'll see how you like that, you impudent monkey!"

Sam's companions looked at each other in alarm. The Deep One was the worst dungeon of all. It was deeper than any of the others and there was no window. Men had been known to go mad in the Deep One. They lost all sense of time and could not tell day from night.

Sam said, "What luxury! To get away from these noisy wretches!"

He winked at them again but they saw fear in his eyes. No one as young as Sam had ever been locked in the Deep One.

"Right!" cried the gaoler and he unlocked the door and held it open. "Are you coming out or do I have to come in and get you?" His small eyes gleamed with malice and Sam knew that this cruel man had the power of life and death over him.

"I'm coming," he said.

His companions wished him well but their expressions were sombre.

Jake followed Sam down a flight of stone steps which seemed to go on forever. At the bottom the gaoler opened the heavy oak door and pushed Sam in. He slammed the door and turned the key.

"So!" he cried. "Let's see if you are still worthy of the name Smiler when you get out of there! If you ever do!" And he left Sam to consider his situation.

The dungeon was in total darkness. It smelt damp and it was very cold. Sam shivered. Then he said aloud "Well, Sam, you've done it now and no mistake!"

He tried to laugh but could find nothing amusing in his plight. He could starve to death in this miserable hole and no one would be any the wiser. If his sister did enquire after him she would be told simply that she could not see him. The gaoler's word was law.

He began to investigate his cell, stepping it out to find how big it was. Five steps to the right and four to the left. He reached up but the ceiling was out of reach. He felt around in the darkness but there was no bed; not even a rough bench. He would have to sleep on the wet straw that covered the floor.

He waited for his eyes to become accustomed to the darkness but they never did. "Must be way below ground," he said.

The sound of his own voice cheered him a little as he leaned back against the wall. "How will I know which day it is?" he wondered and suddenly, for the first time, he was really frightened.

"Stop it, Sam!" he told himself sternly. "You will not be brow-beaten by that ferret of a gaoler. Sing, boy! Sing!"

He sang all the songs he knew but the words echoed eerily. When he had finished singing he counted to a thousand and repeated the alphabet twenty times.

"Is it night yet?" he wondered.

Eventually he sank down on to the ground and slept.

He was woken by a slithering noise over his head. "What the devil?" he cried.

There was a crash and then someone fell on top of him, making him cry out.

His first thought was that he must be dreaming. He was in the Deep One and there was only one way to get in or out. That was through the door which was securely locked. He shook his head to clear his thoughts and rubbed his eyes.

A girl's voice said, "Damn and double damn!"

A girl? In the Deep One? Sam was astonished. "That was me you fell on," he cried. "Who the devil are you?"

"Gee, I'm sorry. Did I hurt you?"

There was something about the voice he couldn't place. A foreign accent maybe? "What's your name?" Sam asked again. "And how did you get in here?"

"I fell in," she told him impatiently. "Ma told me to watch my step but I didn't. It's the story of my life!"

"You fell through the ceiling?" he echoed. "But that's impossible."

"Not for me, it isn't!" She laughed and he was glad she wasn't hurt.

She went on. "I fell off a horse in France and nearly drowned in the Thames. In Munich a car backed into me and - "

113

"A car? What is that?" There was a moment's silence. "You don't know what a car is?" she demanded, her tone incredulous. "Oh come on! You've got to be kidding!"

Sam was annoyed but intrigued. A car? He had never heard of such a thing. "So what is it?" he repeated.

She ignored the question. "Was this some kind of a dungeon?" she asked.

"It's called the Deep One," he told her, "but what I don't understand is – "

"The Deep One? Oh, that's terrific!" She sounded very friendly and he wished he could see her but it was too dark.

"But they should have a notice up," she said. "A warning or something. I could have broken my leg! Oh! This place is fantastic. I must take a photograph for the folks back home. If I haven't broken my camera."

"Camera?" he repeated. "First a car and then a camera. What language do you speak?"

"If you mean where was I raised then the answer's Kansas, the greatest little state in the whole U S of A."

"U S of A?" he echoed.

"Smile please!"

Smile? Sam was beginning to think she must be mad. "You're talking in riddles," he began but was silenced by a sudden flash of light. It

114

only lasted a second or two but by its light he saw a girl about his own age. She was wearing what looked like a pair of chopped off breeches and a sort of shirt with short sleeves. She was holding a small contraption to her eyes and there was something very odd about her.

"What have you done?" he asked. "Why have they put you in here?"

"Nobody put me in here," she told him. "I told you. I fell in."

"Now you take one of me," she said. "No one back home is going to believe that I fell into a genuine dungeon." She pronounced it "gen-you-wine".

She thrust something into his hands and guided his finger to what felt like a small button. "Press that!" she told him and when he did there was another flash.

She said, "My name's Mary-Lou Denton and I'm doing Europe with my ma and pa. They've been crazy to come to England. What's your name?"

"Sam Tyson. I'm in here for stealing a loaf of bread."

Her laughter rang out. "Oh, I get it!" she said. "You're kind of acting the part. To make it more real. Gee, that's really cute, Sam. Now how do we get out of this dump."

Sam was just beginning to say that they did

not get out when he heard the door creak. A shaft of light lit up the darkness, making him blink.

She said, "Hey, come on Sam. Take my hand. We'll make it."

Sam could not understand what was happening but the door was certainly open. He found himself following her up the stairs into the daylight.

To his amazement they walked right past Jake Wicket who was lolling in a chair and seemed unaware of their existence. The girl ignored the gaoler and a moment later they walked out through the main gates into the street. Sam looked back at the gaol which towered above them.

"What a shame they let it fall down," she said. "Still, I guess it makes a nice old ruin."

Sam was so excited to be free he hardly listened to her. The street was exactly as he remembered it. A donkey cart lumbered along laden with straw. A young girl sold oranges from a basket: "Oranges! Come buy!" An elderly gentleman rode by on a splendid white horse which picked its way daintily among the rubbish which littered the street. A beggar woman sat at the roadside, her hand outstretched for alms.

It was so good, thought Sam, to be out in the world again.

In the daylight Mary-Lou looked ridiculous in her strange clothes but now she was looking around her. "Why are these places always so crowded?" she grumbled. "Oh! There's a hot-dog stand!" she told him. "I'm starving." She looked at him admiringly. "That outfit's terrific!" She told him. "And the make-up, too. They've made you look dirty and half-starved. If I didn't know I'd say you came straight from the seventeenth century!"

"But this is the seventeenth century – " he began but now she was waving to someone.

"Hi Ma! Pa! I'm over here."

He looked, curious to know what kind of parents could have produced such an odd daughter but he could see no one who might possibly be her mother and father.

She frowned. "They can't see me and Pa's a little deaf. I'll have to go. But it was real nice meeting you, Sam." She smiled and then darted away – and then, as he watched her go, she faded into nothing.

Just vanished before his eyes! Sam shook his head, thoroughly confused.

"Mary-Lou Denton," he repeated. "From Kansas? Now where the devil is Kansas?" And what was that camera thing that flashed – and what in the name of blazes was a hot-dog?

He shrugged. "Who cares?" he asked himself

with a broad smile. "I'm free, thanks to Mary-Lou."

Whistling cheerfully he set off to find his sister. Somehow he had escaped from the Deep One and with a little bit of luck he need never go back.

BARNET'S
REVENGE

Barnet's Revenge

As the church clock struck midnight the tombstone shuddered and then tilted to one side. Moonlight shone on to the cold stone so that the words were clearly visible.

John Stanley Barnet, 1964 – 1980,
Rest In Peace

The grass parted as the soil cracked open and the head of a boy appeared. The rest of his body followed.

John stood on his grave and brushed himself down. Then he turned to look at the wording on the headstone. As he did so his eyes hardened.

"Rest In Peace!" he muttered. "That's a laugh! How can I rest in blooming peace when I shouldn't have been there if it hadn't been for that stupid oaf Luckford!"

He sighed heavily then stretched his cramped limbs and brushed himself down again. He still wore the clothes he had been buried in – sneakers, jeans and a tee shirt. John (better known as

Barnet) was sixteen – and would never be seventeen.

"Rest in peace!" he repeated grimly. "If I have my way it will be his turn to kick the bucket! People like him are a menace to society. If anyone should be dead and buried it's him!" He smiled grimly but there was no humour in his eyes. "Now where shall I find the wretch?" he wondered and decided to try 'the Dog and Bone'.

He went into the crowded pub and leaned against the bar. Sure enough he saw his murderer sitting at a table with Andy Briggs and looking very pleased with himself. He was drinking a pint of beer as though butter wouldn't melt in his mouth.

Sam Luckford was a no-good double dealing crook – in Barnet's opinion. He was also a fat slob. He ate too much, drank too much and never did an honest day's work. Barnet had never liked him, even before the murder.

"Yes, it was murder!" whispered Barnet. "The jury thought it was an accident but Luckford and I know better." He knew that Luckford had deliberately run him down. And why? So that he couldn't tell the police what he had found out about Luckford's shady dealings.

Oh yes! Barnet had overheard it all. How Luckford patched up badly damaged cars and

122

resold them to innocent people; cars that weren't safe to drive. Barnet had heard him boasting about it to Andy Briggs.

Suddenly Luckford glanced towards the bar and he saw Barnet. The shock made him spill his beer – all down the front of his dirty shirt and shapeless trousers.

"That's a good start!" said Barnet and he winked at Luckford. Luckford's mouth fell open and his hand shook so much that he had to put down his glass.

"What's up with you?" Briggs asked him. "You look as though you've seen a ghost!"

"I have!" whispered Luckford and he pointed towards Barnet. All heads now swivelled in Barnet's direction but no one else could see him.

"There's no one there," said Briggs. "You really are a wally sometimes. Get on with your beer."

"But he's there!" cried Luckford. "I can see him as plain as I can see you! The boy – the boy in the accident. John Barnet. He's standing there, looking at me!"

"Never!" said Briggs. "You're having me on!"

Luckford's pasty face now turned a nasty shade of grey. "I tell you it was an accident," he told Barnet in a trembling voice. "I swear it was. They found me innocent. I was acquitted!"

"Not by me," Barnet told him. "I knew better and I found you guilty!"

By this time everyone was staring uneasily at Luckford. The atmosphere was no longer jolly and behind the bar the pub's owner began to get annoyed.

"Get your friend out of here," he told Briggs. "He's upsetting my customers."

Grumbling to himself Briggs persuaded Luckford to leave the bar and together the two men stood in the deserted car park.

"Now look what you've done!" grumbled Briggs. "Got us thrown out, that's what!"

Barnet had followed them out and now he stood in front of them. Slowly he raised the forefinger of his right hand and beckoned to Luckford to follow him.

"No!" cried Luckford, visibily shaking. "No, no, no! I'm not coming anywhere with you! You get away! Leave me alone."

"What are you on about?" asked Briggs, thoroughly confused. "Look, if you don't pull yourself together I'm off."

"No," cried Luckford again, terrified of being left alone with the apparition. He clung to Briggs' arm. "It's that boy! The one I knocked down. There! Right in front of you. He's come back to haunt me."

"But why should he? You didn't mean to kill him. It was an accident, wasn't it?"

"Of course it was. I swear to God it was!"

Barnet wagged his finger reprovingly at this lie and Luckford groaned. Briggs stared round the empty car park. "Look, there's no one here," he said. "So pull yourself together. I'm off. See you some time."

In spite of Luckford's efforts Briggs tugged himself free and ran to his car.

As he drove off it occurred to Luckford that he could escape by the same means. He made a dash for his own car and leaped into the driving seat. He put it in gear and roared wildly out of the car park into the road.

"Thank heavens for that!" he muttered. "Blasted kid!"

Suddenly a face appeared in the rear view mirror and Luckford saw that Barnet was sitting in the back seat. He screamed with fright and almost lost control of the car but with a desperate wrench of the steering wheel he somehow saved the situation.

"What do you want?" he blubbered. "I never meant it. Honest I didn't. It was an accident."

"It was murder!" said Barnet grimly. "Now drive to your second-hand car lot – and no funny business on the way or you'll live to regret it."

There were seven shiny cars standing in a row.

125

Barnet made his companion get out of the car and inspect them. They all looked perfectly respectable but Barnet knew better. "Now choose one of them," he told Luckford.

"But why?" stammered Luckford.

"Because we're going for a little ride," Barnet told him.

Luckford shuddered and began to protest but Barnet insisted. Finally Luckford pointed to one of the cars.

"So that's the safest one," thought Barnet. He shook his head. "I don't like the colour," he said. "Choose another."

Luckford's trembling finger moved again.

"No," said Barnet. "I don't like the shape. Try again."

Every time Luckford selected a car Barnet found some reason to reject it until at last there was only one car left.

"We'll go in this one," said Barnet cheerfully.

"No!" cried Luckford.

Barnet looked at him in amazement. "But why not?" he asked innocently.

"Because it – because I – " Luckford looked at his tormentor helplessly.

"You don't mean it's not safe to drive, do you?"

"N-no but – I mean – "

Barnet's smile was cold as ice. "Get in!" he said.

The terrified man began to plead but Barnet put a finger to his own lips to silence him.

They sat side by side as they drove out of the town, over the bridge and along to the cliff path that overlooked the beach. They parked the car on top of the cliff, facing the edge.

"Now," said Barnet, "we're going to let the car roll towards the edge of the cliff."

Luckford turned several shades paler. "I won't!" he cried. "Are you crazy? We'll both be killed!"

Barnet laughed. "You forget," he said gently. "I'm dead already."

"Then I'll be killed!" cried Luckford.

"Of course you won't," said Barnet. "Because at the last moment you'll put the brakes on, won't you?"

"The brakes? Oh, but they're not – I mean –" He was unable to go on.

"You don't mean the brakes are no good!" said Barnet. "Oh surely not! You'd never sell a car with faulty brakes, would you? That wouldn't be honest, would it?"

Luckford opened and shut his mouth but no sound came out. He looked like a dying fish, thought Barnet and he leaned over and released the handbrake.

The car rolled slowly forward and Luckford pumped frantically at the brakes. They did not work and the car toppled off the cliff into the sea.

A week later the headstone above Barnet's grave had been straightened. Beside it a new grave was covered with flowers.

The inscription on the headstone read:

Samuel Charles Luckford. 1950 – 1989
Gone But Not Forgotten

Luckford's elderly aunt stood alone beside his grave. "Poor dear Sammy," she whispered. "What a dreadful tragedy. He was such a good boy!"

Just for a moment she fancied she heard a boy laughing but when she turned she was still alone.

THE
VILLAGE SCHOOL

The Village School

The school stood on the right-hand side of the lane, in the shadow of an old oak tree. The playground surrounded it on all sides and was enclosed with a crumbling brick wall and rusty railings. There was an inscription set in the brickwork of the front wall – St Benedict's School, Built in 1889.

"A hundred years old!" muttered Maggi. "What a dump!"

She stared at the weeds which flourished everywhere and then glanced up at the roof. Several tiles were missing and there was a bird's nest in the top of the chimney.

So this was the village school, she thought with dismay and her heart sank. Her mother had warned her that the village school would be very different from the large school she had attended in London but this was worse than she expected.

With a sigh she pushed open the creaking gate and walked up to the door. This had once been painted blue but the colour had faded and the paint was flaking off.

She stepped in reluctantly and found herself in a cloakroom. The only washbasin was chipped and a large piece of yellow soap seemed to have been nibbled by rats!

She wanted to turn and run. Instead she tried to make a joke of it. "Well, St Benedict," she said, "I don't think much of your school and that's the truth!"

There was a row of coat hooks on the wall but no coats. As she stood there, trying to pluck up courage to go on, she heard the scrape of chairs and the clatter of desk lids closing.

She opened a door and stepped into the classroom.

There were no children in the room but the teacher was standing behind a tall narrow desk, covering the blackboard with small, spidery writing. She was tall and thin and her greying hair was twisted into an untidy bun at the back of her neck. She turned briefly in Maggi's direction and said, "You're late! Write your name in the Late Book."

"But –" Maggi faltered. "I'm the new girl. This is my first day. I thought –"

"It's over there."

Maggi followed the pointing finger and found

a ledger full of names on the wide window sill. There was a pen and ink-well beside it and she obediently added her name to those on the last page.

"Are you Mrs West?" she asked nervously. She had been told to ask for the headmistress.

"I'm Miss Pilcherd." She turned irritably. "Sit down and get on with your work."

"Yes Miss Pilcherd. Er – which is my desk?"

Apparently exasperated by this, Miss Pilcherd threw down the chalk. "Questions! Questions!" she cried. "Can't you think for yourself, child? Take the empty desk." She pointed again and Maggi took the desk next to the old black stove.

The desk was broken but Maggi was not going to risk further trouble so she sat silent and apprehensive. How on earth had she got herself into such an awkward predicament, she asked herself miserably. Presumably she had come into the school by the wrong door. She should have asked for the headmistress right away. When the rest of the children came back from wherever they were she would ask one of them the way to Mrs West's room.

She began to study the writing on the board.

LAUNDRY WORK – Clothes should be sorted into different piles.

1) Soiled whites should be soaked over-
night in a tub and may need the use of
a dolly peg.
2) Very soiled articles must be boiled in
the copper.
3) Coloured articles must be rinsed sepa-
rately adding:
a) laundry blue for whites
b) ox gall for browns and greys. . .

It all sounded very odd but Maggi thought she
had better make an effort. In her school bag she
found a biro and a notebook and began to copy
down the notes.

From the playground outside she heard a
new voice: "Feet apart – jump! Together –
jump! Apart! Together. And stop. Heads up,
stomachs in. In, I said, John! That's better.
Now arm swinging over the head and back,
with me – Begin! Mary Wetherby, where are
your shoes?"

"At the menders, miss."

"See me at playtime."

"Yes, miss."

Maggi was beginning to feel that something
was not quite right about St Benedict's. It was so
old fashioned! She could not – would not– stay
here. She would tell her mother how hopeless
it all was. She would make her understand.

There was a small convent school in the next village which might be better. It couldn't be any worse!

Suddenly she became aware that Miss Pilcherd was standing over her, a long thin cane held in her hand.

"Is that all you have written?" she demanded ominously.

"But I've only just started!" Maggi protested.

"I will not tolerate laziness in my class. Do I make myself clear?"

"Yes, but –"

"Yes Miss Pilcherd! Do I have to teach you manners as well?"

"No but –"

"No, Miss Pilcherd! Hold out your hand, miss, and we shall see whether or not I can teach you manners!"

Shakily Maggi rose to her feet, unable to believe her ears. She was searching for words of protest when the teacher caught hold of her hand and brought the cane down hard across her knuckles.

Maggi let out a sharp cry of pain and anger – and at that moment the teacher's outline began to fade! Her lips were moving furiously but there was no sound. The cane rose again but before it could fall both teacher and cane became shadowy and transparent.

Then they were gone.

Maggi stared around the empty room incredulously. "But that's impossible!" she whispered.

She glanced at the blackboard and saw that the teacher's spidery writing was fading. Soon that too was gone.

"I didn't imagine it!" she told herself. "I know I didn't!"

With a supreme effort of will Maggi marshalled her chaotic thoughts and fled from the building. She stood in the sunlit lane, trembling violently with shock.

"I didn't imagine it!" she repeated. "She was there! She was real!"

Suddenly she glanced down at her hand and her heart seemed to miss a beat. Across her knuckles there was an angry red weal!

It was a moment or two before Maggi could think sensibly but it finally dawned on her that the empty building she had just left so hurriedly could not be the school she was meant to attend. The grim old building was obviously the original St Benedict's .. Presumably she would find the new school further along the lane.

Weak with relief she walked on and sure enough, as she rounded the corner, she saw a modern building with a neat board outside.

St Benedict's School. Headmistress, Mrs West.

"Thank Heavens for that!" she murmured and took a deep breath before going in.

Mrs West was a plump, cheerful woman and she listened to Maggi's story in amazement.

"That must have been the old headmistress," she told Maggi. "Miss Pilcherd. Of course, the children all called her Fishy but never to her face. Isn't that incredible! You saw her ghost! You must be psychic or something. She taught quite a few of the older villagers and they still talk about her. A proper tartar, by all accounts." She looked at Maggi's hand and made sympathetic noises. "We must get some antiseptic cream for that nasty weal."

Maggi said wonderingly, "I could believe in the misty sort of ghosts but that cane really hurt! I still can't believe it actually happened."

A gleam came into the head mistress's eye and she suddenly went to the door and called to her secretary.

"Mrs Burton will know all about Miss Pilcherd," she told Maggi. "She's lived in the village for most of her life."

Mrs Burton's story about the former headmistress was tinged with sadness.

"She was fixed up to wed a soldier," she told them, "but he never came back from the war. She never got over it, poor soul, and she never looked at another man. It turned her nasty and bitter inside. My mother says she was a sweet-natured girl before he was killed but then she went sour and took it out on the kids. They all hated her."

"What happened to her?" asked Mrs West.

"She drowned herself in the village pond," the secretary told them. "One day in June, I believe it was. That caused a stir, by all accounts. It's deceptive, that pond. It's not very big but it's very deep in the middle. Mind you, she was getting on for sixty then and some said she was mad. But my mum didn't think so. Just twisted up inside with grief."

Maggi sighed. "I'm beginning to feel quite sorry for her," she said. "Has anybody else seen her ghost or is it only me?"

Mrs Burton laughed. "You seem to be the only one. Now I wonder why that is?"

Mrs West looked thoughtful. "It might be the anniversary of the day her young man died." She smiled at Maggi. "Maybe you could do a bit of investigating. Ask around in the village. Perhaps you would write an account of what happened for the school magazine. I'm sure the whole village would find it fascinating."

Maggi said she would. Then she followed the headmistress along the corridor to her new classroom.

Maggi wondered if she would enjoy life at the new St Benedict's School but as she greeted her new teacher she reminded herself that it would certainly be a vast improvement on the old one!

THE SIGH

The Sigh

"We were just passing the little wood at Spark's Corner and we thought we heard something," I told him. "A sort of sigh. It was so scary. We turned and ran. Then we felt a bit daft so we went back. Jo thought it might be an old tramp but I said if it was a tramp why didn't we see him? It wasn't dark or foggy or anything. I reckoned it could have been a hedgehog. They do make funny noises. We had one once that used to come into the garden at night and sometimes it huffed and puffed and sometimes it sort of snored."

"Never mind all that," said the desk sergeant. "Just get on with the story."

I took a deep breath but before I could continue my brother Jo took up the tale. He was only nine then – two years younger than me.

"We went back," he said "and stood in the same place and at first there was nothing but then we heard the sound again. A long, deep sigh. A sad sort of sigh. Almost a groan. As though someone was in terrible trouble or despair. We began to look around but still couldn't

143

find anything and we were just going to give up when Anne saw the blood."

The desk sergeant stopped writing and gave us both a funny look. To me he said, "You're quite sure it was blood, miss?"

"Well, it was definitely red," I said, "and it looked like blood to us. It was sort of frothy – a little patch of it, soaking into the grass. It wasn't sticky as though it had been there for a long time. It looked very fresh."

He gave a sort of laugh and said, "You an expert on blood, then?"

Jo looked at me and I shrugged. "We both watch the telly," I said. "They tell you things like that sometimes." I felt like sighing myself. It was obvious he didn't believe a word of it.

He turned back to me. "So you saw what you thought was fresh blood. What happened next?"

Jo said, "We found another patch of blood and then a whole trail of it, leading deeper into the wood. We followed it and that's when we saw the young man lying against the tree. Sort of propped up against it. He wasn't breathing and we knew he was dead. Didn't we, Anne?" I nodded and he went on. "There was a knife sticking out of him and blood all over his clothes and the other man, the older man, was digging his grave. At first they didn't seem to see us but then the older man turned towards us."

I said, "His face was terrible." I shuddered at the memory of that face and started to cry – I couldn't help it – and Jo put his arm round me. Just quickly because he had seen it too and he knew it was true. The policeman did not like me crying. He said sternly, "No need for that, miss," and went on writing while I dried my eyes. Then he asked, "Terrible in what way, miss?"

I could see it so clearly, "Very pale and his mouth trembled. He was sweating and his hair seemed to stand up on end. He didn't speak to us but he sighed again and kept shaking his head as though he didn't know what was happening. He stopped digging and wiped his face with his sleeve. Jo said to him, 'What on earth have you done?'"

Jo nodded. "But he still didn't speak. When he had finished digging the grave he started to –"

"Hang on!" grumbled the policeman. "You're going too fast. I'm not a blooming computer, you know." He glared at his biro, shook it, tried to write with it and threw it down in disgust. "Always the way," he remarked. "Always run out while you're in the middle of something."

He found another one and looked at Jo. "Now, where were we? Ah yes. The grave. What makes you so sure he was digging a grave? Could have been digging a big hole."

Jo looked at me.

I said, "Hole, then. He pulled and tugged the body into the long, narrow 'hole' and then he covered it all with earth. I suppose that made it seem rather like a grave. I mean he didn't actually put up a headstone but we got the general idea —"

The policeman's good humour deserted him. "Now don't you start getting clever with me, miss," he said. "Let's have a description of these two characters. First the murderer."

He grinned as he said the word "murderer" to let us know he was treating the whole thing as a hoax. Once again Jo and I exchanged hopeless looks. Now we were really in difficulty. The description of the murderer would sound so unlikely. Jo cleared his throat and said, "He was tall with — longish hair."

"How old, would you say?"

"About sixty, maybe."

"The pensioners strike back!" said the policeman but we didn't feel like laughing. "Dark or fair or bald?"

"He wore a wig," said Jo. "A long curling wig to his shoulders." Before the policeman could say anything he rushed on. "He wore knee breeches and a white shirt with a lace cravat and his coat was —"

The policeman paused in mid-sentence and drew his brows together. Then he laid down the biro and screwed up the report he had been writing.

"Out!" he said. "Not another word. Just get out."

"But sir –" I cried.

"Out I said. And don't come back."

"But isn't anyone going to check out our story?" I gasped.

"No, miss, they are not." He glared at us and jerked a thumb towards the door. "My men have got more important things to do than chase around in the woods –"

"But we aren't lying! God's honour!" I cried. "We can take you right to the grave!"

"Out! Before I throw you out! Curling wig be blowed! You must think I blew in with yesterday's rain!"

We left. There was nothing else to do. We talked it over and decided not to mention it again. In a way I was glad. I wanted to forget the whole thing as quickly as possible.

All that happened twenty years ago. Yesterday I read in *The Times* that a dog had unearthed human bones in that very same wood. With the aid of scientific equipment they had dated them. It seemed that the bones belonged to a young man and they were about three hundred years old. That meant that whoever it was had died towards the end of the seventeenth century.

I thought about it for a long time and then I rang my brother. He's married now and he works in a garden centre. "Jo? How are you?"

We chatted and then he said, "Have you seen the account in *The Times* about the bones in Sparks Wood?"

"Yes I have," I told him. "That's why I'm ringing you now. I don't understand it at all. We saw it happen about twenty years ago but they say it happened three hundred years ago! It doesn't make sense. I mean, we saw it happen."

There was a long silence. I said, "Jo? Are you still there?"

"I'm here," he said. "I've been thinking. We did see something happen but was it the actual murder? Or a recreation of the murder?"

"I've wondered about that," I told him. "But Jo, we saw fresh blood."

"Or a re-creation of fresh blood. Or a manifestation of fresh blood. Whatever you like to call it."

"I don't know. . . ."

"Look," said Jo, "it was a long time ago and we were only children. Perhaps we were at a very susceptible age. Sensitive to the supernatural. We could have seen ghosts."

"Ghosts! They were very solid ghosts then!"

"We probably wouldn't have known exactly what we were seeing."

"But we didn't only see them," I reminded him. "We heard them, too. We heard the older man sighing." I shook my head.

"We should have gone back that same day. We should have looked for the body. Marked the spot somehow. If only I'd thought to take a photograph. If only we'd had some kind of proof. I knew right from the start that nobody was going to believe us. I'd just like to understand what happened," I said. "I feel I'd like to set the record straight."

"Write to the newspaper," he suggested. "Tell them what happened to us. Tell them what we saw. After all, they only know he died. We know he was killed. They won't know who he was or why he was killed but at least it will be another piece of the jigsaw falling into place."

I thought it was a good idea and went to bed planning how I would word my letter to *The Times*. Next morning I wasn't quite so sure. What good would it do? We couldn't save the young man's life. Maybe I should let them rest in peace.

I never did write the letter.

I wrote this instead.

The Hardy Boys
Mystery Stories

ARMADA

Nancy Drew Mystery Stories

Nancy Drew is the best-known and most-loved girl detective ever. Join her and her best friends, George Fayne and Bess Marvin, in her many thrilling adventures available in Armada.

ARMADA

The Chalet School
Series

ELINOR M. BRENT-DYER

Elinor M. Brent-Dyer has written many books about life at the famous alpine school. Follow the thrilling adventures of Joey, Mary-Lou and all the other well-loved characters in these delightful stories, available only in Armada.

Other titles by
Enid Blyton
in Armada

ARMADA

Enid Blyton
School Stories
in Armada

Malory Towers series

First Term at Malory Towers	£2.99	☑
Second Form at Malory Towers	£2.99	☐
Third Year at Malory Towers	£2.75	☑
Upper Fourth a Malory Towers	£2.75	☐
In the Fifth at Malory Towers	£2.75	☐
Last Term at Malory Towers	£2.75	☐

St. Clare's series

The Twins at St. Clare's	£2.75	☐
The O'Sullivan Twins	£2.75	☑
Summer Term at St. Clare's	£2.75	☑
Second Form at St. Clare's	£2.75	☑
Claudine at St. Clare's	£2.75	☐
Fifth Formers at St. Clare's	£2.99	☑

ARMADA